Is Mandie really alone?

"IT'S NOT REALLY dark in the woods yet, because there aren't any leaves on the trees," Mandie told herself. "If I go down the road, I'll be late and Mama will be wondering where I am. It'll only take a few minutes to get through the woods."

She paused a moment longer and then, grasping her books in her arms, she ran into the woods. Dry leaves and twigs crackled and popped under her feet. The farther she went, the darker it grew.

"Oh, where is that field?" she whispered as she tried to see through the trees ahead to the open field she knew was on the other side.

Suddenly there was a loud screeching noise— like someone screaming—and then an ear-splitting pounding filled the woods. Mandie froze in her tracks, her heart trying to jump out of her chest.

"What is that?" she cried.

Don't miss any of Mandie Shaw's
page-turning mysteries!

And look for the next book, coming soon!

The Secret in the Woods

Lois Gladys Leppard

BANTAM BOOKS

NEW YORK • TORONTO • LONDON • SYDNEY • AUCKLAND

RL: 2.6, ages 007–010
THE SECRET IN THE WOODS
A Bantam Skylark Book / June 2001

Mandie® and A Young Mandie Mystery® are registered
trademarks of Lois Gladys Leppard.

ISBN: 0-553-48717-5

Visit us on the Web! www.randomhouse.com/kids

**Educators and librarians, for a variety of teaching tools,
visit us at www.randomhouse.com/teachers**

Published simultaneously in the United States and Canada

BANTAM SKYLARK is an imprint of Random House Children's Books, a division
of Random House, Inc. SKYLARK BOOK and colophon and BANTAM BOOKS and
colophon are registered trademarks of Random House, Inc. Bantam Books,
1540 Broadway, New York, New York 10036.

PRINTED IN THE UNITED STATES OF AMERICA

OPM   10   9   8   7   6   5   4   3

For my great-niece,
Tessla Smith,
with love

1

The Noise

THE SEVENTEEN PUPILS in Mr. Tallant's school were quietly studying arithmetic problems, reading, or creating drawings to show at the upcoming open house for parents and friends. Nine-year-old Mandie Shaw was sketching her kitten when she heard the door open and looked up to see Dr. Woodard enter the schoolroom.

"Mr. Tallant, how are you?" the doctor said as he walked toward Mr. Tallant's desk.

Mandie tried to listen to their conversation, but the two men spoke in tones too low to understand. She glanced at Joe Woodard, the doctor's son, and saw that he was smiling at her.

Then Dr. Woodard turned and motioned for Joe to follow him out. Joe hurried by Mandie's desk. "Got to go to town," he whispered. "See you in the morning." He grabbed his coat and hat from the pegs at the door and left with his father.

Mandie sat there for a moment, twirling her pencil as she pondered Joe's remark. What were they going to town for? she wondered. Joe had not said anything to her that morning when they had walked to school together.

Joe Woodard had walked Mandie to and from school every day since she had begun three years before. Mandie couldn't remember a single day when he hadn't been there. Now she would have to walk home by herself. Charley Gap in Swain County, North Carolina, was a small community. None of her other classmates lived out on the road where she and Joe did. Mandie's inquisitive nature wouldn't let her rest until she met him the next morning and found out what his journey into town was all about.

At least her friend Faith could walk with her for a few minutes before turning off on the road to her home. Faith Winters and her grandmother, Mrs. Chapman, were living with Miss Abigail while their house was being repaired.

When the going-home bell rang that afternoon, Mandie rushed to get her coat.

"I'm ready," Faith told her as she put on her coat and hat and reached for the books she had laid on the bench nearby. Her long brown hair spilled over her shoulders.

"Let's go," Mandie replied with a big smile, leading the way out the front door.

As soon as the two reached the road and all the other pupils had gone in the other direction, Mandie asked, "Did you see Dr. Woodard come in and get Joe? Joe whispered to me that they were going into town. Can you imagine why his father would get him out of school to go to town?"

"Of course I saw Dr. Woodard," Faith replied. "They probably went shopping," she added as they walked down the road.

"Shopping? Do you think Dr. Woodard would get Joe out of school just for that?" Mandie asked as they hurried along in the cold wind.

"Mandie, doctors don't have normal schedules and lives like the rest of us. They have to do things whenever they have a break," Faith replied.

"I know," Mandie answered, pulling her collar up around her neck. "But I can't imagine what they would be shopping for."

"Whatever the stores in Bryson City sell," Faith reminded her. "That's what they'll be buying."

"There aren't very many stores in Bryson City," Mandie remarked.

"I suppose you could ask Joe tomorrow about what they bought," Faith said as they came to the crossroad where she turned off. She suddenly stopped and looked at Mandie. "Are you not taking any books home? What about homework?"

Mandie stopped too and looked down at her hands. She stomped her feet. "Oh, Joe Woodard is the cause of that! I forgot my books!"

"How can Joe be the cause of your forgetting your books?" Faith asked.

"Because *he* always carries my books and I forgot to get them," Mandie said. "Well, I suppose I'll have to go back." She turned back up the road.

"Better hurry or Mr. Tallant may be gone," Faith said as she went on her way.

Mandie kept mumbling to herself as she ran back toward the schoolhouse. "Mr. Tallant, please still be there. I have to do my homework. Please, please, don't be gone already."

She finally reached the building and ran up onto the front porch and pushed open the door. Mr. Tallant was still there.

As Mandie rushed inside to her desk, Mr. Tallant looked up from the pile of papers before him. "Did you forget something, Amanda?"

"Oh, yes, sir, Mr. Tallant," she said, trying to get her breath as she picked up her books. "These," she added. "Goodbye, I'm going to be late."

"Goodbye," Mr. Tallant called after her as she hurried back to the door.

When she got to the road, Mandie realized the sun was already setting, half-hidden behind the Nantahala Mountains. "Oh, I've got to hurry before it gets dark," she said as she continued down the road.

When she came to the crossroads where Faith had left her, she paused. If she cut through the woods she could get home much quicker.

"It's not really dark in the woods yet, because there aren't any leaves on the trees," Mandie told herself. "If I go down the road, I'll be late and Mama will be wondering where I am. It'll only take a few minutes to get through the woods."

She paused a moment longer and then, grasping her books in her arms, she ran into the woods. Dry leaves and twigs crackled and popped under her feet. The farther she went, the darker it grew.

"Oh, where is that field?" she whispered as

she tried to see through the trees ahead to the open field she knew was on the other side.

By the time she reached the center of the woods, it was so dark she could barely see her way to keep from running into trees and bushes. She had to slow down.

Suddenly there was a loud screeching noise— like someone screaming—and then an ear-splitting pounding filled the woods. Mandie froze in her tracks, her heart trying to jump out of her chest.

"What is that?" she cried. She wondered which direction to go in to avoid whatever it was. The pounding ceased abruptly for a moment and then began again, this time softer.

She finally got her feet unglued, and holding her breath, she ran as fast as her short legs would carry her. As she ran, the noise gradually became fainter and she realized she was getting away from whatever it was.

At last she sighted the dried-up cornfield through a thinning of the forest ahead. Trying to run faster, she finally left the woods. Rushing to the middle of the field, she collapsed on the hard frozen ground, dropping her books.

"Oh, thank you, God, thank you," she managed to whisper as she looked up at the darkening sky.

Taking a few deep breaths, Mandie gathered her books and managed to get to her feet. She glanced behind her at the woods, afraid she would see someone or something in pursuit, but there was no sound and no sign of anyone.

Within minutes Mandie was across the field and onto her father's property. Her father was usually at work on the split-rail fence he was building around their property line. But he was not there today.

Without letting up, Mandie rushed to the back door, flung it open, closed it behind her, and practically slid across the kitchen floor to sit in the warmth of the big iron cookstove. Her kitten, Windy, jumped out of the woodbox and came to rub against her and purr. Her mother looked up from her work at the kitchen table.

"You need to get your homework done before supper, Amanda," Mrs. Shaw told her as she continued to mix ingredients in a bowl.

"Yes, ma'am," Mandie said. She removed her gloves and hat, unbuttoned her coat, and then rose to go hang them on the pegs inside the parlor door. Coming back, she picked up her books. "Where is Irene, Mama?"

"I sent your sister to the smokehouse after a piece of fatback," Mrs. Shaw said, straightening up to look at Mandie. "Did your sister leave school early? You're always home before she is."

"No, ma'am, I don't think she did," Mandie said in a shaky voice. She didn't dare let her mother know she had cut through the woods. "I was delayed a little bit." She started toward the parlor door before her mother could ask any more questions. Then she stopped at the doorway. "Where is Daddy?"

"He's been over at Mrs. Chapman's all afternoon working with the other men on her house," Mrs. Shaw replied.

Mandie went on into the living room with her books and sat in a chair near the blazing fire in the fireplace. She was still cold, both from the weather and from the fright she had endured. Windy followed her and curled up on the hearth. Opening her arithmetic book with shaking hands, Mandie began her homework.

She was so absorbed in her lessons that she didn't realize her sister had entered until Irene spoke.

"Well, Mandie, what were you doing in the woods?" Irene asked as she came to sit on a nearby stool.

"In the woods?" Mandie repeated, looking with surprise at her sister.

"Yes, in the woods," Irene replied. "I saw you come out of the woods and then fall down in the old cornfield."

"You saw me come out of the woods?" Mandie asked, playing for time.

"Yes, that cornfield is in plain sight of our smokehouse, you know," Irene said. "Looked to me like you were running from something. When you just sat down there in the field, I thought at first you might be hurt and I started to come see. But then you got up and took off toward the house. What were you doing in those woods, all alone and in the dark so late in the day?"

Mandie did some quick thinking. She couldn't always trust her sister not to tell on her.

"If I tell you why I was in the woods, would you not tell anyone? Promise?" Mandie asked.

Irene shrugged. "Why would I tell anyone that my sister was dumb enough to go into those dark woods alone?"

Mandie breathed deeply to keep from becoming

angry with Irene. She closed her blue eyes for a moment. "Joe had to leave school early today," she began.

"I know," Irene muttered as she picked up the poker and poked at the logs in the fireplace.

"Well, because of that I had to walk home by myself. Where were you after school?" Mandie asked.

"You walked through those woods because you had to walk home alone?" Irene asked, ignoring her question. "That's a poor place to go alone. Even I wouldn't venture in there in the dark by myself."

"Well, it so happened I forgot my books and had to go back to get them and—" Mandie started to explain.

Irene laughed. "You forgot your books and had to go back to get them? You know we always have homework."

Mandie sighed. "Irene, you know Joe always carries my books. I walked with Faith to the crossroads and then realized I had forgotten my books and had to go back and get them. Then I thought I'd take a shortcut through the woods so I wouldn't be late getting home. That's all. Now are you satisfied?" She was annoyed with her sister's interrogation.

"Well, why didn't you say so in the first place?" Irene asked, standing up.

"Because I didn't want Mama to know I had come through the woods alone, that's why. And I figured if I told you, you would tell her." Mandie was speaking in a louder voice.

"I don't always tell Mama everything," Irene said. "And neither do you. You don't tell her sometimes when I meet Tommy Lester." She started toward the door to the kitchen and looked back. "I won't tell her, but I'd advise you to stay out of those woods."

"Thanks, Irene," Mandie replied in surprise. Her sister was not usually so cooperative.

Irene went on into the kitchen. Mandie opened her arithmetic book again, but her mind wandered.

She could still hear that terrible noise in the woods. Shivers ran down her spine. Maybe she would tell Joe about it tomorrow and the two of them could investigate. There was definitely something going on in that dark place.

2

Surprise

THE NEXT MORNING Mandie rushed through breakfast and was waiting at the road when Joe came by to walk to school with her.

"Well, good morning," Joe greeted her as she went to meet him. "You're out early this morning, for a change." He grinned. "I usually have to wait for you."

"Oh, Joe, I have things to talk about," Mandie said with a frown. "Let's go. I'm cold."

The two started their daily walk to the schoolhouse. Joe carried Mandie's books.

"There was this awful noise in the woods yesterday and I was afraid to wait and investigate," Mandie began. "You see, I was—"

"You were in the woods yesterday?" Joe interrupted. "What were you doing in the woods?"

Mandie looked up at the tall eleven-year-old boy. "*You* were the cause of it all. I—"

"*I* was the cause of it all?" Joe asked in a loud voice. "I didn't have anything to do with your going in the woods."

"Oh, but you did," Mandie said firmly. She stuck out her chin. "You always carry my books and yesterday you left early and I forgot my books and had to go back and get them and then I was going to be late so I cut through the woods." She took a breath. "*That's* how come I was in the woods."

"Mandie!" Joe looked exasperated. "Don't forget that I'm two years older than you and I'll finish Mr. Tallant's school two whole years ahead of you. You'll be left here for two years by yourself. Are you going to remember to carry your books then?" He grinned down at her.

Mandie bit her lip. "Well, anyhow, when I got halfway through the woods there was this scary noise, like someone screaming and pounding on something," Mandie replied. She wrapped her arms around herself as she walked. The sound was still vivid in her mind.

Joe stopped and touched her on the shoulder to slow her down. "Mandie, you should never, never go in those woods alone," he said. "Goodness knows what you heard. You could have been harmed! Do you understand? Never go in the woods alone again."

"Don't worry, I don't plan to," Mandie replied, scooting away from his hand and continuing to walk. "But I wanted to know if you would go with me so I could look around and see if I could figure out what that noise was all about."

Joe pulled her to a stop. "Mandie, I'm sure whatever that was will be gone by now," he said. "There is no reason to go poking around."

"But I'd like to know what it was," Mandie said. Looking up at him, she added, "It could have been some poor hurt animal."

Joe hesitated. "I suppose we could go look and see if that's what it was. But, mind you, we are not going without my rifle. I'll hurry home after school tomorrow and get it."

"Tomorrow? Can't we go today?" Mandie asked.

"No. My mother has to measure me for some new pants we bought in town yesterday and do some alterations," Joe replied.

"So you went to town to buy pants yesterday?" Mandie asked.

Joe grinned at her. "Yes, that's right. Seems

I'm outgrowing all my pants, so we bought some new ones that could be taken up and then let back down later."

"Faith thought y'all were going to shop in the stores in Bryson City," Mandie told him. "Did you buy anything else?"

"No, we didn't," Joe answered. "We went to my father's tailor and that's all."

"Why didn't the tailor alter the pants for you?" Mandie asked.

"Mr. Dargan had so many orders ahead of ours that I would have had to wait weeks. My mother knows how to alter them. That way I could have a new pair to wear in a few days. You see, the bad weather we've been having this winter kept people from traveling into town, and then when it finally began to thaw and clear up, just about everybody went," Joe explained as they walked on down the road.

"Just about everybody except me," Mandie said with a frown. "My mother promised to take Irene and me into Bryson City one day. Soon, I hope." Mandie skipped a step to keep up with Joe's long legs. "About tomorrow. Where do we meet after you go and get your rifle?"

"You go home from school and I'll go to my house, get the rifle, and come by your house to get you," Joe suggested.

"That won't work, Joe. If I go home my mother may have chores for me to do and I'd have to ask permission to go," Mandie objected. "Can't you just take your rifle to school?"

"No, you know Mr. Tallant wouldn't allow that," Joe said. "But you could go home with me to get it—that is, if you can walk real fast so it won't take so long."

"I can keep up with you," Mandie said, squaring her shoulders. "That's a better idea."

"Then I can tell my mother where we're going," Joe said.

"Why?" Mandie asked.

"So someone will know where we are just in case we run into trouble, Mandie," Joe explained. "Someone should always know where you are."

"The woods aren't that far off," Mandie said as they turned into the lane to the schoolhouse. "In fact, they join my father's property."

"I know," Joe said. "I wonder why your father doesn't buy up all those woods since it connects with his property?"

"He can't. Nobody knows where the owner is," Mandie explained.

The two entered the one-room schoolhouse, hung their coats and hats on the pegs at the door, and went to their desks. No other pupils had arrived.

"Good morning." Mr. Tallant smiled at them from his desk at the front of the large room. "You're here bright and early. I wonder if y'all would do me a favor." He stood up with a stack of papers in his hands.

"Yes, sir," Mandie and Joe answered together.

"I have the drawings and posters some of the students have made for our open house. If y'all could hang these all around the room, I'd appreciate it."

Joe stepped forward and took the papers. "Yes, sir."

"How do we hang them up?" Mandie asked, looking around the log walls.

"You will find pegs and hooks that we put up years ago for such stuff," Mr. Tallant explained. "We haven't used them in a few years." He walked over to a wall and pointed at a hook. "See? There's one."

"There are some high ones and some low

ones," Joe told Mandie as the two started around the room. "You do the lower ones that you can reach and I'll hang the higher ones."

Mandie began hunting for hooks where she could hang the papers Joe had given her. "Have you decided when we'll have this open house, Mr. Tallant?"

Mr. Tallant, seated back at his desk, replied, "It's so hard to plan anything in the wintertime because of the weather. But I thought spring ought to be at least on its way in a couple more weeks . . . so what do you two think about a Saturday in late March or early April?"

"Yes, sir," Joe said, reaching to stick a drawing on a hook. "The weather ought to be better by then."

"What all will we be doing for this open house?" Mandie asked as she continued hanging the papers.

"I'll let you two in on a surprise," Mr. Tallant said with a big smile.

Mandie and Joe instantly stopped to look at him.

"Miss Abigail has asked me if we would like to have that old organ she has in her back room," Mr. Tallant went on. "It's old but it's still in perfect shape and I told her definitely yes, just as soon as I can round up some men to move it."

"Oh, then we can have music," Mandie said, delighted.

"But where are you going to put it? Will it fit in here?" Joe asked, looking around the room.

There were four groups of pupils in Mr. Tallant's school, one group in each corner.

"Since we won't be using the organ except when the whole school can get together, I thought I could move the group where you sit, Joe, up a little closer to the next group and keep shoving desks closer together all around the room. That should give us plenty of space," the schoolmaster explained.

Joe grinned. "I'll be glad to help, Mr. Tallant, whenever you're ready."

"Thank you, Joe. I knew you would," Mr. Tallant replied. He looked up at the sound of voices outside the front door. "What do y'all say we don't mention this organ until I have the whole class together?"

"Yes, sir," Mandie and Joe said together as they put the last papers on the wall and went to their desks.

The door opened and Esther Rogan and

Faith came in. Close behind them was Irene, with Tommy Lester trailing. They all began hanging up hats and coats. The rest of the school's pupils entered behind them.

Esther walked down the aisle toward her desk, looked around the room, and announced loudly, "Guess what? Miss Abigail is going to give us her old organ. Faith just told me. Won't that be wonderful, having music?"

Mandie, Joe, and Mr. Tallant looked at each other and smiled.

Well, that was at least one secret she didn't have to keep anymore, Mandie decided.

Mr. Tallant stood up. "Since you all know about the organ now, we might as well move the desks around to make room for it, if you boys will all help."

The schoolmaster directed the placement of the desks. The boys, wanting to show their muscles, shooed the girls away when they tried to help.

Finally Mr. Tallant stood back and surveyed the rearrangement. "Now, I believe the men may be able to move the organ for us right after school tomorrow. I would like to ask the boys if they would hang around while they do it in case we need to relocate any of the desks."

"Yes, sir," said all the boys, including Joe.

"Not tomorrow, Joe," Mandie whispered across the room to him.

Joe raised his eyebrows. "Sorry, what can I do?" he whispered.

Now she and Joe would not be able to go explore the woods after school tomorrow because of the organ. She tried to think up some excuse that Joe could use to get out of staying to help but couldn't come up with anything that she thought he would accept.

If they didn't go tomorrow to find out what was going on in the woods, whatever it was would probably be gone. Should she go back by herself and risk running into trouble? She had no idea what had made all that noise. No, she didn't believe she could get up the nerve to walk into those woods again by herself. And there was no one to ask except Joe.

When school let out and Mandie and Joe were walking home, Mandie brought up the subject again.

"If you are going to stay after school, when

will we be able to go to the woods?" Mandie wanted to know.

"Maybe the next day, Mandie. You know there's no way I could get out of helping Mr. Tallant. We can still go later," Joe said.

"And later whatever that was I heard will probably be gone and I'll never know what it was," Mandie argued.

"You don't have to know everything that goes on in this world, Mandie," Joe told her. "Some things sometimes are better left alone."

Mandie took a deep breath as they continued down the road. "All right, all right, then we will go the day after tomorrow. Just don't forget," she said, relenting.

"How could I forget?" Joe asked with a big grin.

"I just hope whatever it was doesn't leave the woods before we can find it," Mandie mumbled.

3

Plans Are Made

THE NEXT MORNING Mandie met Joe at the road to walk to school. The weather had warmed up a little and the sky was clear, although the sun had not yet peeped over the Nantahala Mountains.

"My father will be using his wagon to get the organ from Miss Abigail's today," Mandie told him as they began walking.

"Not alone. It's too heavy for one man," Joe replied. "Who is helping him? Do you think he might need me? I could get out of school a little early to go with him."

Mandie looked at her friend, her blue eyes twinkling. "Oh, no. That's already arranged. Esther's father, Tommy Lester's father, and Mr. Miller are all coming to help move it."

"Do you think that's enough? An organ is awfully heavy," Joe replied, frowning.

"Of course it is," Mandie told him. "My father knows what he's doing. I'm going to stay after school until my father brings in the organ and then I'll ride home with him, just in case you want to come with us."

"All right," Joe agreed. "I'll do that. I suppose the other men will meet him at Miss Abigail's and leave their wagons or horses there. So he'll have to take them back to her house to get them."

"I suppose so," Mandie said, taking bigger steps in order to keep up with Joe's long legs.

"Your father may end up taking Faith and Esther and Tommy to Miss Abigail's too," Joe said.

"I suppose they will all wait after school until the men get the organ moved into the schoolhouse," Mandie said. "I wish I knew how to play the organ. Maybe we could take lessons from Miss Abigail."

"My mother used to teach piano and organ," Joe reminded her. "Remember, she has played at church when the pianist was out."

The schoolhouse came into view up the road and Mandie suddenly remembered what she had wanted to ask Joe. "Are we going to search the woods tomorrow after school?" she asked.

Joe took a deep breath and said, "Oh, Mandie, if you insist."

At that moment Mandie's sister, Irene, came hurrying past them on her way to school. "Y'all better hurry up," she called to them as she continued down the road. "You're going to be late." She didn't even glance back.

"Yes, we'd better get a move on here, Mandie," Joe said, walking faster. "We sure don't want to be late."

Mandie quickly caught up with him. "Don't forget," she said. "We're going to see if we can find out what made that noise, tomorrow, after school."

"All right, all right, come on," Joe urged her.

The two rushed inside and hung their coats and hats on the pegs at the door. Everyone else was already there, talking among themselves.

Faith stood beside her desk. "Miss Abigail has the organ all cleaned and polished and she played it to be sure everything was working," she told Mandie and Joe.

Esther Rogan quickly joined her and said, "All the men are working on Faith's grandmother's house today, but they plan to quit in time to bring the organ."

Suddenly the bell rang to begin the school day. The pupils scrambled for their seats as Mr. Tallant picked up his book to call the roll. The room became silent.

"Good morning, everyone," Mr. Tallant greeted them. As the pupils responded he continued. "This is going to be a wonderful day for our school. Now, does anyone here know how to play the organ? If so, raise your hands, and I'll arrange a schedule for each of you to play when we open the school every morning." He paused and looked around the room.

Mandie watched as her schoolmates looked at one another. If anyone knew how, they were not going to admit it.

"Now, I'm sure some of you must play the organ. How about doing your classmates a favor and volunteering? Anyone?" Mr. Tallant waited but the room remained silent. "All right then. Here's the way we'll do this. When I call the roll, each of you answer yes or no, whether you know how to play the organ or not. Is that understood?"

"Yes, sir," the students murmured.

As the schoolmaster called the names, the replies were almost unintelligible. He didn't ask them to repeat their answers, and Mandie wondered how he would know what to record in his book. She noticed that quite a few replied "No, sir" in a loud voice, and she knew those students really didn't know how to play an organ.

When Mr. Tallant got to Mandie's name down in the S's, she replied, "No, sir, but I would like to learn." Everyone turned to look at her.

"That's fine. We'll see what we can do about that," Mr. Tallant told her. "In fact, I'm thinking of adding organ lessons to our regular schedule if we can find someone to teach it."

"Miss Abigail plays the organ and the piano," Faith said.

Mr. Tallant smiled at her. "I know, but she made me promise that I would not ask her to teach if she donated the organ. However, she is looking around for a teacher for us."

Mandie could hear several of her friends blow out their breaths. Evidently music lessons were not very interesting to them.

"Now, let's get started," Mr. Tallant told them as he put the roll-call book on his desk and picked up several sheets of paper. "Group Four, y'all continue reading Shakespeare from where we left off yesterday. Group Three, do Test Number Two in the back of your English book. Write the answers on a sheet of paper with your name on it. Group Two, continue with your arithmetic from yesterday, and Group One, I'll help you with your handwriting exercise."

Joe was in Group Four with the older students and Mandie was in Group Three, next in age. She quickly opened her English book to find Test Two in the back. It was three pages long, but that would not take much time. As she worked her way through the nouns and pronouns and their verbs, her mind wandered to the woods. Who could it have been in the woods? She knew everyone in the community. No one had mentioned being in the woods.

At recess Mandie ate her lunch with Joe and Faith in a corner in the back of the room. She decided she should tell Faith about her shortcut through the woods.

"After I left you and got my books on Monday, I took a shortcut through the woods to get over to the cornfield next to our property," Mandie began in a low voice as she glanced around to be sure no one else was listening.

Faith leaned forward as she bit into her ham

biscuit. "You cut through those woods by your-self?"

"Yes, but I won't do it again," Mandie told her. She explained about the noise she had heard. Then she glanced at Joe. "I got Joe to promise to go back in there with me so I can find out what it was."

Joe spoke up as he swallowed the last bite of his biscuit. "I don't know what good it will do. Whatever it was will be gone by the time we go back, but Mandie insists."

Faith smiled. "Yes, wherever there is even a hint of a mystery, you can be sure Mandie won't rest until she solves it."

Mandie sighed. "But there might be someone hurt in there, or maybe an animal trapped, or something. We need to find out. Do you want to go with us? We're going after school tomorrow."

Faith shook her head. "No, I don't think I can. I'm helping my grandmother with some needlework in the afternoons this week."

"Maybe your grandmother would let you come over to my house Friday and spend the night and we could talk about this," Mandie said.

"I doubt that I can Friday, but maybe Satur-day I could. I'll ask her," Faith promised.

"Joe, do you think you could come spend Saturday night too?" Mandie asked.

"Well . . ."

"If I ask my mother about y'all coming to spend Saturday night, she'll bake a nice big chocolate cake," Mandie said with a teasing grin.

"Oh, yes, in that case I'll be there," Joe said quickly.

"Me too," Faith added.

The bell rang for classes to resume and everyone quickly packed away their lunch things and returned to their desks.

The day passed slowly for Mandie, but finally her father and the other three men arrived with the organ. Mr. Tallant dismissed the pupils, saying that anyone who wanted to could go on home but that he hoped some of the boys would stay in case they were needed to move things around.

Mandie glanced around the room. No one was going home. Everyone wanted to wait and see the organ. Her father came in and spoke to Mr. Tallant.

"Everyone please stand over on that side of the room," Mr. Tallant said, indicating the area where they had moved the desks. "Stay clear of this space here where the organ is going to be set."

The pupils hurried to get out of the way. Mr. Shaw went back outside, and in a few minutes he and the other three men appeared in the doorway with the organ.

Mandie watched as they gradually rolled the organ into the space Mr. Tallant had made for it. This was an old organ? It looked like a new one to her. But then, everything Miss Abigail owned was fine and well taken care of.

"Just a little bit this way, please," Mr. Tallant directed them, motioning to the left of where he stood. "And not too close to the wall."

The men finally got it placed and stood back to look at it.

"Can someone test it to be sure it's still playing after that journey in the wagon?" Mr. Tallant asked, looking around the room.

Mandie knew he was still trying to find out who knew how to play the organ. Everyone was silent.

"Here, I'll test it for you," Mr. Shaw offered when no one replied. He sat on the circular stool that matched the organ and pumped the pedals. Mandie couldn't see what he was doing, but a melody suddenly came out of the instrument. "It's fine," Mr. Shaw said, standing up.

"Thank you," Mr. Tallant told him. "And I thank all you men for carrying such a load. I know it was terribly heavy."

Mandie was looking at her father. She hadn't known he could play an organ. But then, they had never had an organ or even a piano in their house. She wondered where he had learned.

As soon as everything was back in place, she edged her way through the crowd to look at the organ. With all its pedals and knobs, it looked much more complicated than a piano. She was excited that the school now had an organ, but she wished it could have been a piano, one of those self-players where you put the roll of paper on the rack over the keyboard and then pedaled like crazy and it would play all by itself. That would have been easy.

"Amanda," her father called across the room. "Get your coat. And anyone else who is going to ride with us. We're ready to go." He looked around.

There was a scramble for coats and eventually Mandie, Joe, Faith, Esther, and Tommy Lester climbed into the bed of the wagon. At the last minute Irene came hurrying to join them.

"We'll go back to Miss Abigail's to get the

other wagons and then Amanda and Irene and I will take you home, Joe," Mr. Shaw explained.

The young people wrapped up in the quilts Miss Abigail had sent to cover the organ and the men joined Mr. Shaw at the front of the wagon.

As he drove the wagon out of the schoolyard, Mr. Shaw glanced back. "Miss Abigail's is the first stop. Then how many of you are going on to our house today?"

All the young people shook their heads. "Nobody, Daddy, not today," Mandie told him. "But maybe Saturday if Mama and everyone else agrees."

"I knew we'd be having company for the weekend because I heard your mother say she was baking a chocolate cake," Mr. Shaw teased.

"You see, what did I tell you?" Mandie said with a big grin, glancing at Joe and Faith.

When they arrived at Miss Abigail's, the other men got their wagons. Tommy Lester left with his father and Esther with her father.

As soon as Mr. Shaw stopped the wagon at the back door of Dr. Woodard's house, Mandie reached over to catch Joe's hand. "Don't forget about tomorrow."

"How could I? See you in the morning," Joe

replied, jumping down with Mr. Miller, who worked for Dr. Woodard.

As Mr. Shaw drove on toward his house, Irene leaned toward Mandie. "What are you and Joe up to tomorrow?" she asked.

"M-Me and Joe? Tomorrow?" Mandie stammered.

"I heard you tell him not to forget about tomorrow," Irene said, pouting.

Mr. Shaw glanced back at the girls and smiled. Mandie could tell he had overheard her comment to Joe. But she wasn't going to explain to Irene right now.

"Daddy, do you think Mama will agree to Joe and Faith's spending Saturday night at our house?" Mandie asked.

"I don't know why not," her father replied. "What in this world would we do with that big chocolate cake she is baking without someone to help eat it?"

As he turned the wagon into their driveway and came to a halt at the back door, Mandie remembered how her father had played the organ. Quickly standing up, she asked, "Daddy, I didn't know you could play an organ. When did you learn?"

Mr. Shaw jumped down and the girls followed him. "Oh, I don't know. It was a long time ago when I was young like you. Now I have to see to the horse. I'll be in shortly," he replied.

Mandie sighed. She wished she could hold her father still long enough to get complete answers to questions she sometimes asked him about his own childhood.

Irene led the way in the back door and Mandie followed. She had things all planned out. Tomorrow she and Joe would explore the woods. On Saturday, Joe and Faith would come to spend the night and they would talk about it. She couldn't wait to find out whether there was anything in the woods.

4

The Search

THE NEXT DAY AT school Mandie wished the time away so she and Joe could go investigate the woods. Luckily, Mr. Tallant didn't catch her whispering to herself as she counted the hours and then minutes until school would let out.

She looked at the tall clock standing in a corner at the front of the schoolroom. Its pendulum was swinging back and forth, and in just twenty minutes the clock would strike the hour, signaling that school was over for the day.

"Twenty minutes, nineteen minutes, eighteen minutes," Mandie mumbled to herself as she glanced from the open arithmetic book on her desk to the clock.

Suddenly Mr. Tallant stood up from his desk at the front of the room, tapped lightly with his ruler, and said, "Boys, and girls, may I have your attention, please?"

Everyone straightened up at their desks and looked at the schoolmaster. Mandie listened eagerly.

"Would you all please hurry and get your things together and be ready to leave in five minutes?" he asked.

Mandie glanced at the clock. It was still ten minutes before the hour. He was dismissing them five minutes early. Why?

"I need to go over to Bryson City to order supplies, including music for the organ, and I would like to get going as soon as possible," the teacher explained, looking around the room.

"Yes, sir" came from almost all the pupils.

"Now I want to ask you not to come to school early tomorrow morning, because I will be spending the night in Bryson City and will not return until it's time to open at the regular hour. It is still too cold to stand outside and wait for me. In fact, if anyone is a few minutes late tomorrow morning, that will be excused." Then he smiled. "However, don't use that for an excuse just to be late."

"Yes, sir" sounded through the room again.

Everyone had their books together by then and waited for the signal to rush for coats.

"You may all go now. Good day. See y'all to-morrow morning." Mr. Tallant sat down at his desk and got his papers together.

As the pupils rushed for their coats, Joe crossed the room. "Every little five minutes counts," he told Mandie. He picked up Mandie's arithmetic book. "Is this the only book you are taking home?"

"Yes, that and my notebook," Mandie replied, looking at the neat stack of books she was leaving on her desk. "That's all the homework I have."

"Come on," Joe told her. "Remember, we have to go to my house and get my rifle before we go look in the woods."

Mandie quickly followed him to the door. Almost everyone else had already taken their coats and left. Faith was waiting outside.

"I waited to walk to the crossroads with you," Faith told them.

"I wish you could go with us to the woods," Mandie replied, putting on her hat and coat.

"It's going to be a waste of time, Faith," Joe told her. "We won't find anything."

"Joe!" Mandie exclaimed. "You don't know for sure."

Faith laughed. "Well, anyhow, y'all can let me know tomorrow if you meet up with anything and you get home safely." She grinned.

"Oh, Faith, I'm not afraid," Mandie said as the three left the schoolhouse and walked together to the road. "Joe is taking his rifle."

"My dad says I'm pretty good," Joe boasted. "If it's anything big I know I can hit it."

"I asked my mother last night and she says it's fine if you and Joe want to spend Saturday night at our house. So, are you coming?" Mandie asked Faith.

The girls quickened their pace to keep up with Joe's long legs.

"Yes, I asked Grandmother, and she agreed that I could come," Faith replied.

"So did my mother," Joe added.

"Then we'll have a good time doing just whatever we want to do," Mandie said.

Joe looked back down the way they had come. "I didn't see Irene, did you?" he asked.

Mandie also slowed down to look. "No, I don't remember seeing her leave," she said. "But everyone was in such a rush to get out when Mr. Tallant dismissed us early that I imagine she was the first one at the door."

"Well, here we are," Faith said as they came to the crossroads where she turned off. "Don't get lost in the woods," she called back to them.

"We won't," Mandie replied. She and Joe continued on to the Woodards' house.

They went in the back door and found Mrs. Miller in the kitchen. She cooked for the Woodards and lived with her husband in a cabin across the field behind the house.

"You sure got home fast today," Mrs. Miller said, stirring a pot on the huge iron cookstove.

"Mr. Tallant let us out a few minutes early," Joe said, dropping his books in a chair. "I only came home to get my rifle. Mandie and I are going to search the woods for some noise she heard in there the other day." He took down his rifle from the rack at the back door.

"Well now, that could turn out to be dangerous," Mrs. Miller replied, stopping her stirring to look at him. "Does your mother know about this?"

"Yes, ma'am. I've already asked her if I could go and she said it was all right," Joe said. "After all, Mrs. Miller, you know I am eleven years old, going on twelve." He straightened his shoulders.

"Age doesn't have anything to do with danger, Joe," Mrs. Miller reminded him. "Just be sure you stay alert and cautious. We all know there are wild animals in those woods."

"Yes, ma'am," Joe replied. He turned to Mandie. "Let's go and get this over with."

"I'm ready," she said. The two started for the back door.

"Wait!" Mrs. Miller called to them as she opened the oven door and pulled out a large pan of corn bread.

Mandie and Joe stopped to look back.

"Y'all just take a hunk of this corn bread with you," Mrs. Miller said, quickly cutting off a piece of the bread and wrapping it up in a dish towel.

"Corn bread?" Mandie and Joe both said at once.

"Yes," Mrs. Miller said, walking across the room and handing the wrapped bread to Mandie. "He's got the rifle. You carry this."

"But what are we supposed to do? Eat corn bread on the way to the woods?" Mandie asked.

"No, it's not for y'all to eat. It's bait for any wild animal that y'all might encounter in those woods," Mrs. Miller explained. "If one of them comes toward you, just drop the corn bread and run. The animal will stop long enough to eat the bread. It has cracklings in it, so that makes it more aromatic to the animals. Just remember that."

Mandie looked at the wrapped corn bread in her hands. "Will that work, Joe?" she asked under her breath.

"Sure it will," he said. "Come on." Looking back as he opened the back door, he added, "Thanks, Mrs. Miller. If we don't find any wild animals to eat it, is it all right if we do?"

Mrs. Miller smiled at him. "Not until you are clear of the woods, and by then you will be almost back home again. Now, be careful."

"Yes, ma'am," Joe replied, going out the door with his rifle.

"Thank you, Mrs. Miller," Mandie called back as she followed.

Out in the yard Joe asked, "Which direction should we go in?"

Mandie looked ahead. "We need to get into that cornfield near my house and go into the woods from there. That's where I came out."

The two cut across property lines and soon came to the cornfield, where they paused again.

"Now where?" Joe asked.

Mandie pointed ahead and squinted in the

late-afternoon sunshine. "I think I came out of there right between those two huge chestnut trees."

The two walked on toward the woods. When they came to the edge of the forest, they peered ahead into the darkness under the thick trees.

"Now, you stay right with me and don't go wandering off," Joe warned her. "Remember, I have the rifle."

"And I have the corn bread," Mandie replied with a laugh.

"We'll go very slowly in order not to surprise any wild animal that might be lurking," Joe explained as he continued ahead.

Mandie stayed right by his side as they entered the woods. She looked around. It was so dark, an animal could be hiding and they wouldn't see it until they were upon it. She wanted to be sure she stayed right by Joe and his rifle.

"Now which way?" Joe whispered as he paused to look around.

Mandie couldn't exactly remember where she had heard the noise. She had been too frightened to do anything but run. She wouldn't let Joe know this. She would just guess.

"I believe I came from that direction," she whispered, pointing to the left.

"That direction will probably take us out on the other side of the woods where it borders the old road, not the road you came down, Mandie," Joe whispered back.

"Well, you decide then which way to go," Mandie replied. "We probably should have gone around and come into the woods from the other side. That way I'd probably recognize the place."

"It's too late now to go all the way around the road to the other side," Joe told her. "So we'll just have to go slow. Look at everything so we don't get lost in here."

Mandie smiled. "We don't have to go as slow as molasses, you know. That would take us all afternoon."

"All right, we'll just rush through here and then turn and rush through in the other direction," Joe said.

"But not so fast we disturb the wild animals, remember, Joe?" Mandie cautioned him.

Joe blew out his breath. "Oh, this is all a waste of time. Mandie, whatever you heard must be gone by now. Besides, you couldn't even figure out what was making the noise. How do we know what we're looking for, anyway?"

"I'll know it if I hear it again," Mandie answered stubbornly, stomping her foot on the dry leaves.

Joe sighed as he glanced at her and led the way deeper into the woods. Mandie followed closely behind him, holding tightly to the corn bread and hardly daring to breathe as she kept looking behind every tree and every bush.

Mandie was beginning to think they had gone in the wrong direction when she saw a fallen log that looked like the same one she had passed on her way out of the woods that day.

"That looks familiar," Mandie told Joe, pointing at the log.

Joe stopped to look. "You came by that log?" he asked.

"Yes, I'm almost sure," she replied. "So I would have been coming from over there, that way." She pointed to her left into a clump of bushes.

"That way," Joe repeated as he set off in that direction.

The two tramped on through the woods and finally reached the other side near the road where Mandie had entered before. Stopping at the edge, Joe said, "Well, we haven't seen or heard anything yet. Do you want to go back through the woods or go around the road? We can't take too long, you know, or our parents might be worried about us."

"Let's just go back through the woods again," Mandie said. "We can go faster this time because I started from here and I think I can find the way I went."

The two again walked through the woods, listening and watching, but nothing appeared or happened. Then, just as the edge of the cornfield came into view through the trees, there was a sudden rush through the bushes. The noise caused both of them to stop immediately. Joe held his rifle ready.

Mandie's heart beat faster as she looked around. Then she laughed in a shaky voice. "Don't shoot, Joe! Look, there's a baby deer behind that tree!"

Joe instantly turned to look. "You're right," he said. "Let's go on and not scare it."

The two slowly started on their way, but Mandie suddenly stopped. "The corn bread!

Joe, let's give that baby deer the corn bread. It may be hungry."

"You'll have to be careful or you'll scare it off," Joe replied, glancing at the deer still behind the tree.

"It's watching us. Let's just put the corn bread down right here and when we go on, it'll come and eat it," Mandie declared, stooping to dump the corn bread out of the towel into a clear space on the ground.

The two went on and finally turned to glance back when they were almost out of sight of the corn bread.

"See! It's eating the bread," Mandie whispered happily as she watched the animal nibble.

"All right, let's go," Joe told her.

Mandie caught up with him as they finally left the woods and were back in the cornfield.

"I told you whatever it was would be gone by now," Joe reminded her.

"We don't know for sure it was gone. It just might not have made any noise while we were in there," Mandie replied.

"Well, at least that's over with," Joe said with a sigh as he walked on across the cornfield.

"But I want to go back again," Mandie replied as she caught up with him. "I know there was something in there. Maybe you and Faith and I could come back again on Saturday when y'all stay at my house." She looked at him, hoping he would agree.

"Maybe, but I won't promise," Joe answered. "Besides, Faith may not want to go into those woods."

"I'll ask her," Mandie said.

She immediately made plans for Saturday. She was pretty sure Faith would agree to come with them to investigate the woods.

Rolling up the dish towel as she walked, Mandie was glad she had had the corn bread to feed the baby deer. It was probably hungry. She would ask her mother for corn bread on Saturday to take with them into the woods again. That baby deer might still be there, and she could at least feed it if she didn't find the source of the noise she had heard.

5

The Mystery at the Schoolhouse

THE NEXT DAY, which was Friday, Mandie's plans were changed. When she met Joe at the road to walk to school, he had news for her.

"My mother says I can go to your house after school today and stay for the weekend instead of waiting until tomorrow to come over, if it is all right with your mother," Joe told her as they walked down the road.

"Oh, Joe, that's good news," Mandie said with a smile. "How did that happen?"

"My father wants to go over the mountain this afternoon to see some elderly patients, and my mother is going with him to take some food," Joe explained. "Of course the Millers will be at our house and I wouldn't be alone if I didn't come to your place, but I'd much rather come visit y'all."

"Oh, yes, of course," Mandie agreed, skipping

a step or two. "Maybe we can talk Faith into coming over this afternoon too."

It so happened that the two met Faith at the crossroads on her way to school. When Mandie asked if she would come on over today, Faith replied, "Well, I have helped my grandmother quite a bit this week already. I would like to go to the singing at the church tonight. Are y'all going?"

"I had forgotten all about that," Mandie said as they walked on toward the schoolhouse. "I don't know if my parents are planning on us going or not."

"I forgot too," Joe said. "But I'd like to go."

"Why don't you come on over to our house this afternoon?" Mandie said. "I'm sure my father will take all of us."

"I'll have to go home first to get permission from my grandmother," Faith replied.

Joe was walking so fast it was hard for the girls to keep up.

"Joe, I don't know why you're in such a hurry," Mandie complained. "Remember, Mr. Tallant told us not to get to school too early because he might be late opening up."

Joe slowed down. "I'm sorry. I didn't realize how fast I was walking. I suppose I was just trying to hurry up and get to school and then get to your house, Mandie, and ask your mother if I might stay tonight, and then go to my house to get my things and come back." He blew out his breath.

"My goodness, you don't have to do all that," Mandie protested. "You know my mother would never say you couldn't come to our house, so just go home after school, get your things, and come on over."

"All right," Joe agreed. "And, Faith, I could use my mother's cart and come by and pick you up so Miss Abigail won't have to take you to Mandie's."

"Yes," Mandie said.

"All right," Faith replied. "Thank you. That will save a lot of time and trouble."

As they approached the schoolhouse, Mandie noticed some of the other pupils were on the front porch. "Mr. Tallant must not be here yet," she said as the three walked into the yard.

Esther Rogan was in the crowd, and she came to meet them. "Mr. Tallant is late," she explained with a big grin. "Imagine, the schoolmaster is late!"

"But he told us he might be," Mandie reminded her. She saw her sister with Tommy Lester leaning against the rail at the hitching post in the yard.

Irene was two years older than Mandie. She considered Mandie and her friends too young to associate with.

The sound of a horse's hooves came down the road. Mr. Tallant was returning. He dismounted at the hitching post and hurried toward the front door of the schoolhouse.

"Good morning, y'all," he greeted the pupils as he pulled out his pocketwatch and looked at the time. "I see y'all got here a little early after all. At least I'm back on time."

The young people returned the greeting and followed Mr. Tallant into the schoolhouse.

Mandie looked at the clock. Mr. Tallant was not late. In fact, he was about five minutes early.

"Now that we're all inside, would one of you boys come with me?" Mr. Tallant asked, going back toward the door. "I have some supplies in my saddlebags and might need a little help."

"Yes, sir." Joe quickly spoke up and rushed to catch up with him.

As soon as they left the room Esther said, "We were wrong. He wasn't late."

"No, he wasn't," Mandie agreed.

"Nobody had a watch," Tommy Lester said. "We were all just guessing at the time."

"I don't think I would try guessing again," Faith added.

Mr. Tallant and Joe came back into the schoolroom, loaded with packages that they put on the schoolmaster's desk. Then Joe went to his seat.

"Now I have some sheet music," Mr. Tallant said, opening one of the packages and displaying a stack of paper. "When we find a music teacher, I'll pass this around. And in the meantime I have some tablets here that you may have if you are in need of writing paper. And I was able to get a box of pencils." He opened other packages as he talked and displayed the merchandise.

"How much are the tablets, Mr. Tallant?" Tommy Lester asked, raising his hand.

Mr. Tallant smiled and looked around the room. "I am delighted to inform you that these supplies are all free, for whoever needs them. They were paid for by a . . . benefactor. So please feel free to file by my desk and take whatever you need—and I say whatever you need, not whatever you wish. As you know, supplies are expensive and therefore scarce. Now come forward." He stood waiting.

The students began forming a line to his desk. He picked up whatever the pupil asked for and handed it out. Mandie noticed Joe did not get in line. She debated whether to go ask for a new tablet or not. She really needed one. The old tablet was almost used up. Then she wondered who had donated the supplies to their school.

"Are you coming?" Faith asked as she walked by Mandie's desk.

Mandie got up and followed her. "I wonder who donated all of this," she said.

"Probably Miss Abigail," Faith said.

"Or Dr. Woodard," Mandie added. "They are the only two people I know who could afford to do such a thing." And then, whispering to her friend, she added, "And you see, Joe Woodard is not taking anything."

"I know," Faith agreed. "But that's no reason why we can't take what we need to do our schoolwork."

When they reached Mr. Tallant's desk he asked, "What do you need, young ladies?"

"May I have a new tablet? I've already used

both sides of the paper in the one I have," Mandie told him.

"Me too," Faith added.

"Of course," Mr. Tallant replied, picking up two tablets and handing them to the girls. Then he reached for two pencils and held them out. "Maybe you need pencils? We have quite a supply of them here."

"Oh, thank you, Mr. Tallant," Mandie said gratefully as she accepted the tablet and the pencil.

"Yes, sir, thank you," Faith told him. He also gave her a new tablet and a pencil.

As the two returned to their desks, Mandie glanced at Joe Woodard again. He was watching the lineup but had not participated.

"Aren't you going to get anything?" Mandie whispered as she passed his desk.

Joe shook his head. "Not today. I write real small so my tablet lasts a long time. I don't need a new one right now."

Mandie knew what he meant. His handwriting was so small it was hard to decipher sometimes. But it made her wonder if his father had donated the supplies. In fact, she was almost sure of it. She looked at him and whispered, "Your father gave all this, didn't he?"

Joe didn't reply but nodded his head and grinned.

At the end of the day, Mr. Tallant made another announcement. "I must return to Bryson City on business this afternoon and I will not be back until Monday morning," he told the pupils. "And I will say again, please do not come to school early on Monday morning because I may not be back right on the dot to open up. Today I barely made it."

"Yes, sir" sounded around the room.

Then school was out for the weekend. Faith and Joe went to their homes and promised Mandie they would be at the Shaws' house shortly. Mandie walked the rest of the way home by herself. Irene had already run ahead of everyone. She seldom walked with her sister.

Mandie explained to her mother that Joe and Faith would be coming along soon for the weekend.

"And, Mama, are we going to the singing at the church tonight?" Mandie asked as she removed her coat and hat.

"I believe your father is going but I am not,"

Mrs. Shaw replied. "I still have lots to do on the needlework I am helping Mrs. Chapman with." While Mrs. Chapman had been in New York for medical help, the women in the community had been assisting with the needlework that she did for a living.

"Is it all right if Joe and Faith and I go with Daddy?" Mandie asked, stooping to pet Windy, who had jumped out of the woodbox behind the big iron cookstove.

"I suppose so," Mrs. Shaw replied, stirring pots of food on top of the stove.

When Joe and Faith arrived later, the three gathered around the fireplace in the parlor and discussed Mandie and Joe's venture into the woods in search of the noise Mandie had heard.

"All we found was a young deer," Joe told Faith.

"But I know there was something in there that day when I heard the noise, and I'd like to go back and look all around again," Mandie insisted.

"Maybe we could do that tomorrow," Faith suggested. "I brought my books, and I have permission to stay until we go to school Monday morning, so we will have time if you want to go back to the woods."

"I'm staying until Monday morning also, but I don't see any reason to go back looking for something when we don't even know what it is. We might as well be hunting a needle in a haystack," Joe declared.

"It won't take us very long to look through the woods again," Mandie told him. "And if you don't want to go, then Faith and I can."

"Oh, no," Joe quickly replied. "It's not safe for you girls to go in there alone. Suppose you meet up with some wild animal? Or some stranger? No, I'll go with you, but, Mandie, please let this be the last time we go traipsing off into that forest."

"If you go with us this time, I won't ask you again," Mandie agreed. "So we'll just plan on going tomorrow afternoon."

"Now that that's settled, we'll go to the singing with your father tonight at the church," Joe said.

As soon as supper had been eaten, Mrs. Shaw asked Irene to help her clear away the dishes so that Mandie and her friends could get ready to go with Mr. Shaw.

"Nobody asked me if I would like to go," Irene complained as everyone stood up from the table.

"If you would like to go, then get ready and

go on with the others," Mrs. Shaw said. "I can clean up supper by myself."

Irene shrugged. "I don't want to go. Everybody just took it for granted that I wasn't going and I don't like that." She began picking up dirty plates around the table.

"I'm sorry, Irene," Mandie said. "You never want to do anything with me. But from now on I'll try to remember to ask you. And you can always just say so yourself without being asked, you know."

Mrs. Shaw quickly cut in, "That's enough said, Amanda. Now, y'all should be ready by the time your father brings the wagon to the back door. Just don't forget that we have chocolate cake waiting for you when you get back."

"Mmmmm!" Joe patted his stomach.

"Thanks, Mama," Mandie said.

"It's going to be hard to sing knowing all that delicious cake is waiting," Faith added.

Mr. Shaw drove them in the wagon to the church. The road ran by the schoolhouse and the three glanced at it as they went past.

"It looks deserted without Mr. Tallant's light on in there, doesn't it?" Faith remarked.

"Yes, but I imagine he's glad to get away now

and then. I'd hate living in a schoolhouse all the time," Joe replied.

"He doesn't exactly live in the schoolhouse, Joe. You know he has his own room just connected to the schoolroom," Mandie told him.

"I'd say that is in the schoolhouse," Joe argued.

"But he does go away sometimes for the weekend," Faith added. "I imagine he has friends over in Bryson City."

"I do believe I hear the piano playing already," Mr. Shaw said as he turned the wagon into the churchyard.

The young people quickly scrambled down after he parked the wagon. The yard was full of wagons, carts, buggies, and rigs. Everyone in the community must be there, Mandie decided, as she looked around on their way to the front door.

Mr. Shaw led the way and found a pew with enough room for all of them in one of the side sections. Even though they had memorized every song in the hymnal, Mandie and her friends grabbed the hymn books. Soon they were singing "Will There Be Any Stars in My Crown?" so loudly that a few people nearby turned and smiled.

Mandie loved singing and this session lasted for two hours. Then the song leader closed the service with "Till We Meet Again." The three young people greeted friends as the crowd began leaving the church. Esther Rogan and her parents were there, and so were Tommy Lester and his mother.

Tommy looked at them, evidently hoping to see Irene, and then shrugged and went on down the front steps.

"He was looking for Irene," Mandie muttered to her two friends.

"Yes," they agreed, giggling.

Mr. Shaw drove the wagon back, letting the horse set the pace. When they came to the schoolhouse, Mandie squinted through the moonlit darkness. Of course there was no light because Mr. Tallant was away. But she suddenly heard organ music.

"Daddy, slow down a minute!" she excitedly told her father.

"There is music in the schoolhouse!" Faith declared.

"I hear it too," Joe added.

Mr. Shaw slowed the wagon to a stop in front of the building and the music suddenly stopped.

He looked at Mandie and her friends. "Do you think it's possible Mr. Tallant has returned?"

Joe shook his head and pointed to the hitching post. "No, sir, his horse isn't there," he said.

They listened for a few minutes and when there was no more music, Mr. Shaw said, "Maybe I should go knock on the door. He might have had to leave his horse somewhere." He jumped down from the wagon.

"But he would have a light, wouldn't he?" Mandie asked as she and her friends followed her father to the front door of the schoolhouse.

Mr. Shaw knocked loudly several times but there was complete silence inside. "I don't know what we can do tonight. We'll go on home and come back tomorrow to check in the daylight," he told the young people.

Mandie knew he was right. They would come back first thing in the morning and check to see whether Mr. Tallant was back or someone else was in the schoolhouse. Now she would think about this all night and wonder what was going on. At least she had her two friends to discuss it with.

6

In One Hour

WHEN MANDIE AND her friends got back to the Shaws' house, Mr. Shaw took care of the horse and then came inside to join them at the kitchen table for the promised chocolate cake and coffee. Irene had already gone to bed.

"And now that I have everything out for y'all, I think I will retire," Mrs. Shaw said. "Joe, I have put fresh sheets and an extra blankct on the cot over there for you."

"Thank you, Mrs. Shaw," Joe said, glancing at the cot across the kitchen where he slept whenever he came to visit.

"I know you and your friends want to talk among yourselves for a while, but don't stay up too late, now, Amanda," Mrs. Shaw told her.

"We won't, Mama," Mandie replied between a sip of coffee and a mouthful of chocolate cake.

Mr. Shaw finished his coffee. "And I'll leave

you alone too. Like your mother said, don't stay up too late. We'll be up with the rooster in the morning."

Even though they had gone to bed late that night, Mandie and Faith rose before daylight on the short winter day and hurried down to the kitchen, where the aroma of perking coffee had already invaded the upstairs. They left Irene asleep in her bed.

"Good morning," Joe greeted the girls as they came down the ladder.

"Oh, you're up too," Mandie said as she stepped off the last rung.

"Your cat saw to that. She slept at my feet last night and this morning she woke me up purring like a windstorm in my ear," Joe replied.

They all went into the kitchen. Mr. Shaw was sitting at the table drinking a cup of coffee. Windy jumped out of the woodbox behind the stove and came to rub around Mandie's ankles.

"Yes, Windy does wake up early every morning," Mandie said, stooping to stroke the yellow cat's head.

"You girls come on and get a cup of coffee," Mr. Shaw said, rising to get it.

"No, Mr. Shaw, don't bother. I'll get the coffee for the girls," Joe told him, going to the cabinet to take down cups. He filled them and set them on the table.

"Well, we could have waited on ourselves," Faith said with a smile.

"Come on, let's sit down here at the table," Mandie told her. Turning to her father, she said, "Daddy, is it all right if Joe and Faith and I walk over to the school today to see whether Mr. Tallant has come back?"

"Well, since there are three of you together, I suppose it will be all right," Mr. Shaw agreed. "However, if no one comes to the door after you knock, I don't want you messing around there trying to look in windows, or whatever. And if his horse isn't there, you will know he's not there either. Understand?"

"Yes, sir. We'll just go knock a few times and then leave," Mandie agreed. She thought about the woods and decided not to mention that to her father. When they went to the schoolhouse, they could just cut through the forest the way she had done that day after school. It wouldn't take long to look around.

"Don't be gone too long now," Mr. Shaw added. "I'd say an hour is plenty long enough to go there and back. Even if Mr. Tallant has returned, you should come right back."

"Yes, sir," Mandie agreed.

"Yes, sir," Joe and Faith said together.

"From what you told me before, Mr. Tallant has gone to Bryson City and does not expect to be back before Monday," Mr. Shaw reminded them.

"But, Daddy, someone must have been inside the schoolhouse playing that organ last night," Mandie said.

"We won't get involved in that," Mr. Shaw said. "Since we can't get in with the door locked, we will have to wait and inform Mr. Tallant of what we heard."

"Whoever it was got inside somehow," Mandie reminded him. "What should we do if we find the door or window open and Mr. Tallant is not there?"

"You come home immediately and get me. You are not to go inside unless Mr. Tallant is there," her father said.

"Yes, sir," Mandie reluctantly agreed.

When everyone had finished their coffee, Mandie helped her father cook breakfast. Joe and Faith set the table. By that time Mrs. Shaw had come into the kitchen.

"Do you want me to wake Irene?" Mandie asked her mother.

"No, I thought I'd let her sleep a little late since it's Saturday," Mrs. Shaw replied, going over to the stove to take the sausage out of the frying pan and put it on a platter. "And we're pretty well caught up on our chores."

"Then I'll help clean up after breakfast," Mandie said. "Daddy said we could walk over to the schoolhouse to see if Mr. Tallant has come home."

"Just be sure you are back in time for dinner, twelve o'clock sharp," Mrs. Shaw replied, taking the platter of sausage to the table.

"Yes, ma'am. Daddy said he would give us an hour to go over there and back," Mandie replied.

As soon as breakfast was cleared away, the three young people put on their coats and hats and gloves and started out for the schoolhouse. The weather was still cold but the sun was trying to peep out from behind a few clouds in the sky. Charley Gap was a valley between the Nantahala Mountains, which made the daylight hours shorter.

As they hurried along the road, Faith said, "I don't see how someone could be inside the schoolhouse and the door locked."

"Oh, I believe I have that figured out," Joe quickly said. "Somehow they managed to unlock the door to get in, and then once inside they locked the door again so no one would notice."

"But, Joe, someone would notice that the organ was playing," Mandie argued. "Seems to me like they would know the organ could be heard."

"Well, it could have been a prank someone was playing," Faith suggested. "Just to make someone curious like we are, knowing that Mr. Tallant was away."

"You think someone deliberately did this to cause us all this trouble?" Mandie considered this. "I wonder if they relocked the door whenever they left."

When the three came to the lane that led down to the schoolhouse, they paused to listen.

"I don't hear the organ," Mandie declared.

"Or anything else except the usual sounds around us," Joe added.

"If someone is in there they could have seen us coming," Faith told them. "A window on the side of the schoolroom would give them a view of the road we just came down."

"You're right," Mandie declared. "Well, come on, let's go check the door. I don't see Mr. Tallant's horse."

The three looked around the yard as they walked. When they stepped up on the porch, Mandie was ahead of them. She raised her hand and knocked on the door. To everyone's surprise, the door slowly swung inward. It was not only not locked, it had not been shut tightly.

"Oh!" Mandie exclaimed as her hand froze in midair.

Joe quickly stepped up closer to look inside the schoolhouse. "I can't see anyone in there," he said.

"Don't forget, Mr. Shaw said we were not to go inside if we found the door open," Faith reminded them.

"Then I think we should close the door," Mandie said. "It's awfully cold to leave the door open." She looked at her two friends.

"Yes," Faith agreed.

"Sure," Joe added, reaching to pull the heavy door shut. The latch clicked on it and he pushed it to be sure it was securely closed.

"Should we go back to your house now, Mandie, and tell your father?" Faith asked.

"Not yet," Mandie said, turning to step off the porch. "Let's cut through the woods and see if we can find the source of that noise."

"Mandie, remember your father only gave us one hour to get back to your house," Joe reminded her as he and Faith followed.

"We'll be back on time. The woods is a shortcut anyway," she told him.

Mandie led the way back down the road to the woods and the three walked into the forest. She slowly and quietly moved forward, watching carefully for signs of anyone nearby. Joe and Faith stayed close. They were all quiet, and the wind blowing through the trees muffled any sound they made.

As Mandie passed a huge chestnut tree, a baby deer ran across her path before disappearing into the bushes. She turned and motioned to her friends with a big grin. Then she remembered with regret that she had forgotten to bring any corn bread to feed the wild animals.

When she came to the fallen log she had noticed before, she stopped and whispered to her friends, "I'm sure we're on the right pathway.

See that log? I passed it before, and it was not far from here that I heard the noise."

"Now which way?" Joe asked.

Mandie thought for a moment as she pushed a loose strand of blond hair under her hat and looked around. Joe and Faith stood waiting and watching. A chipmunk darted under the fallen log.

"This way," Mandie finally said, walking to her right. She was not exactly sure, but she didn't want her friends to know it.

The three moved cautiously on through the dense trees and bushes. Finally Mandie could see the opening into the cornfield and knew they were leaving the forest again without finding anything. Just then she heard a faint sound way back in the woods.

It sounded like *Ta-dum, ta-dum, ta-dum!* and then abruptly quit. The three froze in their tracks as they listened.

"That was it!" Mandie exclaimed, but instead of going back to investigate, she ran forward into the cornfield and stopped as her friends caught up with her.

"I heard it!" Faith declared breathlessly.

"So did I!" Joe added.

The three stood there, looking at each other, trying to decide what to do.

"We don't have time to go back. Our hour must be up," Joe declared.

"Yes!" Mandie agreed, blowing out her breath. She was secretly frightened and was grateful that Joe had made the decision for her.

"Then let's go," Faith said, starting to walk across the field.

As Mandie and Joe caught up with her, Faith said, "I don't think I want to meet up with whatever was making that noise."

"I can come back another time," Mandie replied, trying to steady her voice.

The three hurried on through the cornfield. The sun had disappeared behind clouds and the day had turned dark and dreary.

"Looks like it's going to rain, anyhow," Joe remarked.

"I'm glad y'all heard that noise. Now you know I wasn't imagining it," Mandie told her friends. "I can't figure out what it sounded like. What could have been making it?"

"It could have been a wild animal of some sort," Joe suggested. "And I didn't remember to bring my rifle. It's good we didn't meet up with it."

"Yes, I'm glad I didn't meet up with it, whatever it was," Faith said.

"Are you going to tell your father?" Joe asked, glancing at Mandie as she hurried on.

Mandie thought for a moment. "I don't think so. Of course, we didn't exactly do anything wrong by cutting through the woods, but I don't see any reason to explain all that to my father. It's enough that we have to tell him we found the door of the schoolhouse unlocked."

"That's right," Joe agreed.

"Mandie, I've been thinking about that," Faith said. "Whoever unlocked the door of the schoolhouse was probably hiding around there somewhere. It could have been dangerous."

Mandie felt shivers run up her spine. She had been secretly thinking the same thing, but she hadn't wanted to admit it. "Oh, they were probably long gone, Faith," she replied. "And if they saw us coming, they wouldn't have wanted to be seen. But I do wonder what they were doing in the schoolhouse."

"They were playing the organ last night, remember?" Joe reminded her, shoving old dead cornstalks out of their way as they tramped on through the field.

"If you call that playing. It was such a strange kind of music, if that's what it was," Mandie said.

"Didn't sound like any music I've ever heard," Faith added.

"When we go back and tell your father that the door to the schoolhouse is unlocked, what do you think he will do about it?" Joe asked as they came to the road on the other side of the field.

"I suppose he will go check everything out and try to figure out a way to lock the door until Mr. Tallant comes back on Monday," Mandie replied as the three stopped at the edge of the road.

"There is more than one key to the schoolhouse, I am sure," Joe remarked. "Seems like I remember my father saying he had an extra key to it for emergencies."

"Do you know where he would keep it? I mean, could we find it so we could lock the door?" Mandie asked.

"I have no idea where to look for it," Joe replied. "That is, if he still *has* a key."

"We could tell my father that your father might have a key, and my father might know where to look for it," Mandie suggested.

"Maybe Miss Abigail has a key," Faith added.

Mandie wondered what Miss Abigail would be doing with a key to the schoolhouse. Joe's father sometimes met with other men in the community on business matters, and they used the schoolhouse for their meeting place. But Miss Abigail was not part of that group.

"I doubt that she does. We could ask your father anyhow, Mandie," Joe said. "He might know who does have a key—that is, if anyone else has one."

"Yes, come on, let's get going. My father will be wondering where we are if we don't hurry and get back," Mandie declared as she started ahead.

She was anxious to relate the events at the schoolhouse and see what her father had to say. The music last night and the unlocked door were all a mystery to her, and she had to solve it somehow.

7

The Missing Key

BACK AT THE SHAWS' house Mandie, Joe, and Faith found Mr. Shaw reading a book by the fireplace. The three excitedly gathered around his chair.

"Daddy, the schoolhouse door was unlocked," Mandie began.

Mr. Shaw quickly closed his book. "You didn't go inside, did you?" He looked at the three sharply.

"No, sir."

"But I pulled the door shut real tight so it would stay closed," Joe said.

"When I knocked on it, it just came open," Mandie explained. "And Mr. Tallant was not there."

"I peeped inside and the room was empty," Joe said.

"Was the key in the lock?" Mr. Shaw asked, frowning as he watched the three young faces.

"No, sir. And we didn't see it anywhere else. Of course we didn't stay to search for it because we came home to tell you what we'd found," Mandie said in one breath.

Mr. Shaw stood up. "I believe I should go investigate."

"May we go back with you, Daddy?" Mandie asked.

Mr. Shaw looked at them. "Well, I suppose you may, but just remember this, you will not go poking into anything at the schoolhouse. I will take care of everything."

"Yes, sir," they chorused.

As they followed Mr. Shaw into the kitchen where he put on his coat and hat, Joe told him, "I believe my father once had a key to the schoolhouse, sir. But he won't be home until late tomorrow and I don't know where it is, if he still has it."

Mr. Shaw nodded. "Yes, I believe your father does have a key, for the community meetings and all that. Do you think Mrs. Miller would know where he keeps it if we were to go by your house and ask?"

"She might," Joe replied.

"All right, then. I'll hitch up the wagon and

we'll circle by your house first," Mr. Shaw decided.

When they arrived at the Woodards' they found Mrs. Miller cooking in the huge kitchen. She looked up in surprise as the group came in through the back door.

"Well, howdy," she said to Mr. Shaw. "What can I do for you?"

"It seems someone has been in the schoolhouse and left it unlocked," Mr. Shaw explained. "We think Dr. Woodard has an extra key that he keeps to open it up when the men meet there. Would you happen to have any idea where he would keep it?"

Mrs. Miller frowned. "Where is Mr. Tallant?"

"He's gone to Bryson City for the weekend. I mentioned it to you yesterday," Joe reminded her.

Mrs. Miller scratched the bun of dark hair coiled at the back of her head. "That's right, I believe you did." Turning to Mr. Shaw, she said, "I don't know that I've ever heard Dr. Woodard say where he kept the extra key, except he did mention one time that he had a secret hiding place for it outside the schoolhouse where he could get it to unlock the door for one of his meetings."

"Think real hard, Mrs. Miller, please," Mr.

Shaw urged her. "Can you remember any little thing about where this hiding place might be? It would have to be someplace that no one would accidentally discover."

Mrs. Miller thought with a huge frown between her dark eyes for a moment, then shook her head. "No, don't believe I ever heard him say a thing about the place he puts it."

"Do you know of anyone else who might know?" Mr. Shaw asked.

Mrs. Miller reached to stir a pot on the stove before the contents could start to burn. "I'd just ask some of the men who go to the meetings at the schoolhouse. They might have seen him get the key or put it back," she suggested.

"I always go to the meetings myself, but I don't remember ever seeing him retrieve a key from a hiding place," Mr. Shaw said. "Come to think of it, I can't remember a time when he wasn't there before everyone else."

Faith spoke up. "Mr. Shaw, Miss Abigail might know."

Mr. Shaw smiled. "Miss Abigail? But she doesn't go to the men's meetings."

"But she always seems to know everything that's going on around Charley Gap," Joe explained.

Mr. Shaw smiled again. "The best thing we can do is go on over there and start searching for the key, which I am sure Amanda is itching to do anyway." He grinned at his daughter.

Mandie grinned back. "I'm sure the three of us can find that key if it is hidden somewhere around the schoolhouse."

"Yes," Joe agreed.

"I'll be glad to help," Faith added.

Mr. Shaw had started to lead the way out the back door when he suddenly turned. "Is Mr. Miller around? He might know something about it."

Mrs. Miller shook her head. "No, he's over helping with the work on Mrs. Chapman's house. He's never involved in those meetings, though. We just work here."

"Thanks, Mrs. Miller," Mr. Shaw said.

Outside, as the group got back into the wagon, Mr. Shaw explained, "I wasn't scheduled to work on your grandmother's house today, Faith. My turn's next Saturday, but several of the neighbor men are there. So if we can't find the key at the schoolhouse, we'll drive over there."

When they arrived at the schoolhouse, Mandie saw that the front door was still closed.

"Nobody has opened it again," Mandie remarked to her friends as they followed Mr. Shaw onto the front porch.

Mr. Shaw paused with his hand on the doorknob. "I'm going inside and have a look around to be sure everything is all right. You three stay right here."

Mandie and her friends crowded in front of the door as Mr. Shaw turned the knob. He pushed but the door wouldn't open.

"Well, now, it looks like someone has locked it back again," he said, turning to look at the three. "Are you sure it was unlocked when you closed it and left?"

"Yes, sir. I know it was, because I was the one who closed it," Joe replied.

"Someone has been here again!" Mandie said in an excited voice.

Mr. Shaw looked down at his daughter. "Someone was probably somewhere around here watching when y'all were here."

Mandie rubbed her hands together as shivers ran down her spine. Someone had been watching them? And probably hearing everything they said, too? That was scary.

"We'll still look for the extra key, just in case someone is inside," Mr. Shaw said. He walked over to a window and tried to look in, but the shutter inside was closed.

The young people waited and watched. Mr. Shaw turned back to them. "Now we'll look for the key," he said. "Stay close to the schoolhouse. Don't go out of the yard." He began searching the high places, like those over the window.

"Yes, sir." The three fanned out across the yard to begin their search.

"Whoever finds it gets two slices of chocolate cake tonight," Mandie declared with a big grin. She stooped to look under the porch.

Joe began searching the outside sills of the windows. Faith began looking in flowerpots sitting around the front porch.

"Don't forget you said that," Joe told her. "Two pieces of chocolate cake!"

They searched for a long time. Mr. Shaw came behind them and searched where they had been.

"Whoever went in there must have found Dr. Woodard's extra key," Mr. Shaw declared as they all stood looking at the schoolhouse.

"Then it must have been somebody who knew where he kept it," Mandie said.

"They could have found it by accident," Joe suggested.

Mandie tried to figure out where a key would be. Then she had another idea. "I wonder if Mr. Tallant takes his key with him when he locks up and goes off somewhere, or does he hide it somewhere around here?" she excitedly asked.

Everyone turned to listen.

"That's a possibility," Mr. Shaw said. "The key is rather large to carry around."

"So maybe the person who unlocked the door found Mr. Tallant's key, and Dr. Woodard's key is still around here somewhere," Mandie suggested.

"But, Amanda, we haven't found a key at all," her father reminded her. "If you're right, it would mean there are two keys hidden somewhere nearby."

"And we haven't even found one key yet," Joe added.

"Joe, think real hard—you too, Faith," Mandie said. "When we were all waiting for Mr. Tallant to get back from his other trip to Bryson City, do you remember where he got the key when he unlocked the door to let us in? Remember, everyone was standing around outside when he rode up."

Joe and Faith looked at her thoughtfully. Mr. Shaw listened.

"He had all those packages and I helped bring them into the schoolhouse," Joe remembered. "I don't remember him getting a key from anywhere, not even from his pocket. He must have had it already in his hand."

"I agree," Faith added. "He rode up on his horse, got down, and came directly to the front door."

"He probably had it in his pocket and you just didn't see him get it out," Mr. Shaw suggested.

"But he had his hands full of packages," Mandie added.

"Did he tie up his horse before he unlocked the door?" Mr. Shaw asked.

"Yes, sir, he did," Joe answered.

Mandie's face broke into a big grin as she rushed across the yard to the hitching post. She quickly ran her hands over the posts and railing. Her fingers came into contact with metal under the post where it connected with the railing. "I've found it!" she yelled excitedly. "I've found it!" She pulled the key out of the crack and held it up as everyone watched.

"I would say that's probably Mr. Tallant's key and we still haven't found the extra," Mr. Shaw said, taking it from Mandie. "Anyhow, I'll go unlock and check inside."

The young people followed him onto the porch and watched as he unlocked the heavy lock and pushed the door open. They crowded into the doorway as he stepped inside and walked around the schoolroom, looking under desks and behind cabinets.

"No one here," Mr. Shaw declared, calling back to the three. "Y'all can come on in if you want to."

Mandie and her friends rushed inside the schoolroom

Everything seemed to be in its place. Mandie walked down the aisle toward the schoolmaster's desk, and then her gaze fell on the round stool in front of the organ. She stopped and pointed. "That stool has been moved. Mr. Tallant always pushes it out of the way."

"You're right," Joe agreed as he came over.

"That's right," Faith echoed.

"But when we heard someone playing the organ, they would have moved the stool to sit down in front of it, so that's probably when the stool was moved," Mr. Shaw told the three. "And we tried the front door when we heard the music and it was locked. Then y'all found the door unlocked and now locked again, so someone has been back in here."

The three sighed in unison.

"You're right, Daddy," Mandie said. "I wonder if it was the same person."

After a few minutes of thinking, Mr. Shaw said, "I believe we should go on back home now. It's probably time for dinner."

The three young people stepped outside on the front porch while Mr. Shaw locked the door.

"What are you going to do with the key?" Mandie asked.

Mr. Shaw tossed the key in his hands and said, "I was trying to decide about that. If this is Mr. Tallant's key and we take it, he won't be able to get inside when he returns. However, if we put it back and it's the one the intruders used, they will be able to use it to get inside again."

The three thought about that for a minute.

"Y'all said Mr. Tallant is not expected to return until early Monday morning," Mr. Shaw reminded them. "What if we take the key and, Amanda, you and Joe could bring it to school with you then to let him in?"

"But what if he gets back before Monday morning? How would he get in?" Faith asked.

"We could leave a note," Mandie quickly decided. "We could stick a note on the door to tell him we have the key."

"I suppose that might work," Mr. Shaw agreed.

"We need to go back inside, Daddy, to get a piece of paper for the note," Mandie told him.

Mr. Shaw opened the door again. Mandie quickly went to her desk, got her notebook, and tore out a sheet of paper. Picking up a pencil, she wrote, *Mr Tallant, we have the key to the schoolhouse in case you come back before Monday morning.*

Mr. Shaw read the note. "All right, that will do. Now we have to figure out how to post the note so it won't blow away." He took the paper and started back outside.

"That's easy," Joe told him, running ahead to point. "There's a hook on the outside of the door that we use for the Christmas wreath. We can just stick it on there."

"Good idea." Mr. Shaw folded the note and bent to push it onto the hook. "That ought to hold." He locked the door and put the key in his pocket.

"Whew! I don't know about y'all but I do believe it must be dinnertime!" Joe declared with a big grin.

As everyone piled into the wagon, Mandie sighed. "We still don't know who unlocked the door *or* who played the organ."

"I'm sure we'll eventually find out," Mr. Shaw said as he shook the reins.

"In fact, we don't even know which key we found, whether it was Mr. Tallant's or the one that Dr. Woodard hides," Mandie added.

"At least we have the schoolhouse all locked up now," Joe said.

"If we keep on investigating, we'll probably answer all those questions," Mandie told her friends.

She didn't intend to let everything drop. She was going to solve the whole mystery, somehow or other.

8

The Secret in the Woods

ON SUNDAY MRS. SHAW had the sniffles and wasn't feeling well enough to go to church. Irene stayed home to help with the noon meal. The three young people went with Mr. Shaw, and on the way home they persuaded him to drive by the schoolhouse to see if Mr. Tallant had returned.

"His horse isn't here," Mr. Shaw remarked as he slowed down to look.

"But, Daddy, don't you think we ought to check the door?" Mandie asked.

"I can see our note still hanging where we placed it," her father replied.

"But don't you think we ought to see whether the door is still locked?" Mandie insisted.

Mr. Shaw finally halted the wagon. "All right, we'll go see."

"I can run up to check the door, Mr. Shaw," Joe offered, standing up in the wagon.

"Go ahead then," Mr. Shaw agreed.

Everyone watched as Joe ran up to the door, tried to open it, and then came back. "It's still locked," he reported.

"But someone could have been inside and locked it when they left," Mandie said as Joe climbed back into the wagon.

"We don't have time for more inspection here right now," Mr. Shaw told her. "With your mother not feeling well, Irene may need help to finish up the noon meal when we get home."

"Yes, sir," Mandie finally agreed. Her father drove on.

Irene had everything ready except setting the table, which Mandie and Faith did. And when the meal was finished, Mandie, Faith, and Joe cleared the dishes away.

Then Mandie persuaded Irene to play checkers with them on the floor of the parlor in front of the fireplace. They needed to have an even number of players so everyone could play in one game together. She and Faith were partners. Irene and Joe beat them badly.

"I'm sorry, Faith," Mandie told her friend. "I suppose my mind was not on the game. I keep wondering about the key to the schoolhouse."

"I'm glad to hear that. Want to play another game?" Joe teased her with a big grin.

"It's only a game of checkers, Mandie," Faith assured her.

"Tomorrow will soon be here and then we'll find out if the key belongs to Mr. Tallant or to Dr. Woodard," Mandie said thoughtfully.

"And don't forget. We must be there early so Mr. Tallant can get in," Joe reminded her.

"You said your father would probably be back this afternoon. Do you think we could go ask him where he puts the extra key?" Mandie asked.

"No, Mandie, because he may or may not be home. And when he does get back, he will probably have calls to make," Joe replied. "Besides, I was invited to stay here until Monday. Are you trying to get rid of me?" He grinned over the checkerboard at Mandie.

"Oh, Joe, of course I want you to stay until tomorrow. I thought we could just run by your house for a minute," Mandie replied.

"But if we did that, I'm sure my mother would find some reason for me not to come back over here," Joe said. "She's real good at thinking up chores for me to do."

"Never mind. I can wait until tomorrow," Mandie told him.

And when tomorrow came, the three friends were early for school. They took the key and Joe unlocked the door. They kept watching from the inside of the schoolhouse for Mr. Tallant to arrive. The weather was too cold to stay outside very long without walking or moving around. Joe had been able to get the huge heater fired up. The schoolroom was warming up comfortably.

The other students began coming in, and when they were all there, Mr. Tallant had still not shown up. Everyone was curious about how Joe had obtained the key and unlocked the door. Mandie and Joe had decided not to divulge their secret. Faith had agreed.

Finally at a quarter past eight, fifteen minutes after the usual beginning of the classes, Mandie heard a horse coming into the yard. She and Joe ran to open the door and look out. Mr. Tallant was hurriedly throwing the reins over the hitching post, and as he turned and started toward the door, he saw them.

"Sorry, but I was a little delayed," he said as he came up on the porch. He looked at the open door and the students inside. "My, my! How did y'all manage to get the door open?"

Joe took the key out of his pocket and held it out as they stepped inside and closed the door. "We found the key at the hitching post," he said.

"The key at the hitching post?" Mr. Tallant asked as he quickly removed his coat and hat and hung them up. "What was a key doing at the hitching post? I have my key." He held it up for them to see.

Mandie and Joe looked at each other. They must have found Dr. Woodard's extra key.

"It was hidden in the crack between the post and the rail," Mandie explained.

And as the three stood there at the back of the classroom, Mandie and Joe told the schoolmaster about the incidents that had taken place during his absence. They spoke low enough that the other students could not hear, although they were plainly curious.

"I had no idea there was a key hidden there," Mr. Tallant told them. "And I have no idea who could have been in the schoolhouse, especially playing the organ. There are very few people in this community who know one note from another, much less how to play an organ." He scratched his head.

"This key is probably my father's, then," Joe told him. "You know he keeps an extra key for when he uses the schoolhouse for meetings."

"Yes, Dr. Woodard does have a key, but I'm surprised he would hide it like that," Mr. Tallant said. "Now I'm late and I see everyone is here and ready for classes, so let's get started." He walked to his desk. Mandie and Joe sat down in their seats.

After the roll was called, Mr. Tallant asked Mandie's group to begin reading aloud while the rest of the students listened and gave remarks.

"Would you please begin, Faith?" Mr. Tallant asked her.

Faith frantically sorted through her books. Her reading book was not there. "I'm afraid I have forgotten my reading book, Mr. Tallant," she said.

"That's all right, Faith," Mr. Tallant said. "Just go sit by someone and share their book. I'll ask Esther to begin."

Mandie quickly motioned Faith to sit by her. Esther began reading and Faith tried to explain to Mandie. "I left my book at your house."

Mandie nodded and whispered back, "We'll get it after school is out."

When school finally let out for the day, Mandie, Joe, and Faith left together. Faith would have to hurry to go to Mandie's house for her book and then get home without being too late.

"We could cut through the woods. It's a whole lot shorter and quicker," Mandie suggested as the three came to the forest.

"All right, but we're not going to stop and search for anything," Joe told her.

Mandie agreed, but she still hoped they would make some kind of discovery as they walked.

When they reached the thickest, darkest part in the center of the forest, Mandie thought she heard an unusual noise, but she couldn't identify what it was. Then suddenly that loud noise she had heard on her first trip through the woods came from nearby. She stopped in her tracks to listen to the high-pitched sound and the rhythmic pounding.

"Joe! Faith!" she exclaimed.

"What is that?" Joe asked.

"It's some strange kind of music," Faith declared.

"Yes!" Mandie agreed. "It's the same music we heard at the schoolhouse when someone was playing the organ, only this time whoever it is is singing!"

"You're right!" Joe agreed.

"Where is it?" Faith asked.

"This way," Mandie said, leading the way into the trees to her left. She walked cautiously through the dead leaves and twigs, trying not to alert whoever was singing. However, she thought they were singing too loudly to hear anybody approaching.

Suddenly they came to a small clearing. Mandie put her hand out to stop her friends. There, standing in the middle of the space, was an old Cherokee Indian, singing at the top of his voice and pounding on a hollow log with a thick stick.

Mandie could scarcely stand still. She wanted to rush up to the old man, but she decided to wait until he had finished. And that took quite a few minutes, as he seemed to repeat different phrases of whatever he was singing in his native tongue. Then suddenly his song ended. The old man bowed to a nearby tree, and when he straightened up he caught a glimpse of the three young people. He started to run.

"Wait! Wait!" Mandie called to him as she

hurried after him. "We just want to talk to you." She managed to catch his jacket sleeve.

The old man squinted down at her, then glanced at Joe and Faith standing behind her. "What?" he asked.

"We . . . we heard you . . . you singing," Mandie stammered. "And . . . and . . ."

"You were the one playing the organ in the schoolhouse, weren't you?" Joe asked.

The old man straightened up. "No wrong. Borrowed white man's music machine."

The young people smiled at his language.

Mandie finally found her voice. "Jim Shaw is my father and he speaks your language. Do you know him?"

The old man squinted his eyes again as he stared at Mandie. "Jim Shaw friend."

The three breathed out together in relief.

"Oh, I'm so glad you know my father," Mandie told him. "We drove by the school and heard you playing the organ when it was locked up. How did you get inside?"

The man hesitated before replying. He looked at each one of the three. "Find key," he said.

"But how? How did you know where it was?" Joe asked.

"Many moons ago, doctor leave key," he replied.

"And I suppose you saw the organ being delivered to the schoolhouse?" Mandie asked.

The man nodded. "Yes, organ make Cherokee music many years ago, when I small like you."

"Oh, I'm so glad we found you!" Mandie kept repeating in her excitement. Then she realized she didn't know the man's name to tell her father. "What is your name? What do they call you?"

"Singing Man," he replied.

"Where do you live, Mr. Singing Man?" Joe asked.

The man pointed to his right. "There, that way," he said.

"Will you show us so we can come back to visit you?" Mandie asked.

The man started walking in the direction he had pointed toward. He led them to the foot of a huge slope of the mountain in the woods. He pushed back thick bushes and stomped through undergrowth, revealing the mouth of a cave. He stopped and pointed.

"A cave!" all three exclaimed as they stood there.

Looking up at the tall man, Mandie asked, "Could we come to visit you one day in the cave?"

"Jim Shaw come visit," he said. "You come, Jim Shaw come."

Mandie grasped his old wrinkled hand. "Thank you," she said. Then she had a sudden idea. Backing up a little so she could see all the way up to the tall man's face, she asked, "No one at our school knows how to play the organ, and we want to have a special day when all our parents and friends come to visit. Please, would you come and play the organ for us?"

"Please," Joe and Faith echoed.

The old man looked at the three. "Only know Cherokee music."

"But that's what we want you to play, your kind of music," Mandie said. "Please say you will. I'll get my father to come and talk to you about it."

Singing Man shrugged. "For Jim Shaw, I do."

At his agreement the three young people suddenly swarmed around him, squeezing his hands and smiling as they thanked him.

"I'm sorry, but I need to get my book and get on home before my grandmother worries because I am late," Faith reminded the other two.

"Yes, we have to hurry," Joe agreed.

Mandie gave the old man's hand one last tug. "I will talk to my father and we will be back." She turned to follow her friends out of the woods. Glancing back, she threw him a kiss, and to her surprise, he threw a kiss back at her.

She was so excited. They had solved the mystery in the woods, the mystery of the key, the mystery of the organ playing in the schoolhouse, and all kinds of odds and ends. She couldn't wait to tell her father what they had discovered.

Mandie's Music Makers

Mandie's new friend, Singing Man, loves music. So does Mandie. If you like music too, try making these special Mandie Music Makers!

Materials you will need
an empty egg carton, plastic or foam
empty baby food jars with lids (cleaned)
plastic eggs (like those used in Easter decorations)
dried beans, such as lentils or limas,
or popcorn kernels
cellophane tape

1. Fill each of your empty containers and plastic eggs with dried beans or popcorn kernels. The number of beans or kernels you use will affect the sound. When you're happy with the number you've used, carefully tape the egg carton shut. Make sure to seal it tightly so that no beans or kernels will spill out once you start shaking. Put the lid back on each baby food jar and screw it shut. Replace the end of each egg and snap it on.

2. Give each music maker a shake. Do you like the sound? Maybe you need to use more beans or kernels—or fewer. Refill and empty as needed.

3. If you like, you can decorate your music makers with glitter, paint, and craft doodads.

Ready? Now make some music!

About the Author

LOIS GLADYS LEPPARD has written many novels for young people about Mandie Shaw. She often uses the stories of her mother's childhood in western North Carolina as an inspiration in her writing. Lois Gladys Leppard lives in South Carolina.

Visit the author's official Web site at www.mandie.com.